THAT'S NOT FAIR

To Ben
To Dafna
(And no "that's not fair" from the rest of you kids)

THAT'S NOT FAIR

By Jane Sarnoff and Reynold Ruffins

BOOKSALE

CHARLES SCRIBNER'S SONS, NEW YORK

Text copyright © 1980 Jane Sarnoff
Illustrations copyright © 1980 Reynold Ruffins
Library of Congress Cataloguing in Publication Data
Sarnoff, Jane.
That's not fair.
SUMMARY: Becky thinks her older brother Bert has
the best of things in their family and "that's not fair."
[1. Brothers and sisters—Fiction]
I. Ruffins, Reynold, joint author. II. Title.
PZ7. S2483Th [E] 80-18983
ISBN 0-684-16714-X

1 3 5 7 9 11 13 15 17 19   R/D   20 18 16 14 12 10 8 6 4 2
Printed in the United States of America

"Nothing to do," said Becky.
"Nothing to do to do to do.
Nothing to play with.
No one to play with.
Nowhere to go.
And that's not fair."

"You have to play with me, Bert," Becky said.
"I don't have anything else to do."

"I'm too busy," Bert said. "As busy as a bee. B-U-S-Y busy."
"That's not fair," Becky said. "I can't even spell."

"Hey Mom. Hey Mom! Hey Mom Mom Mom?" Becky called.
"I don't have anything to do."
"Come on down and help dust the dining room or peel the potatoes,"
Becky's mother said.
"That's not fair," Becky whispered. "Cleaning and cooking is sissy
silly girls' work."

"Better not let Dad or Mom hear you say a D-U-M-B dumb thing like that," Bert said.
"That's not fair," Becky said. "You were listening."
"But you didn't hear me," Bert said. "I was quiet as a mouse."

"Want to take me somewhere anywhere, Dad?" Becky asked.
"I'm busy now, Becky," Becky's father said. "How about cleaning your room?"
"That's not fair," Becky said.

"Everybody is busy but me.
Everyone has things to do except me.
I don't have anything to do.
And now I have to clean my room.
It's not fair," Becky said.

"You always say things aren't fair," Bert said.
"'Not fair. Not fair.'
You say 'That's not fair' when you can't do
what you want to do.
You say it when you are sad and when you are mad.
M-A-D.   Mad as a wet hen.

"Well elephants have four knees and other animals have only two knees.
Only elephants have four legs that bend forward in the middle
the way our two legs bend.
Do you see S-E-E see that?
Other four-legged animals can only bend their
front legs that way
—they only have two knees. T-W-O two.
Do two-kneed animals complain?
Do they say 'That's not fair'? N-O no.
They don't say it because
fair doesn't have anything to do with it.
That's just the way things are.

HOW ANIMALS KNEEL

"And fair doesn't have anything to do with
people being busy or rooms being cleaned," said Bert.
"Not at all. No way.
What's not fair is if there's a chocolate cake and
we're both allowed to have a piece and
I cut the pieces and give you a very little piece
and me a big B-I-G big piece.
That's not fair.
Think about that, Rebecca.
T-H-I-N-K think about that."

"Don't call me Rebecca," Becky said.

"Can Ben come out and play?" Becky said.
"Sorry, Becky," Ben's father said. "Ben's visiting his grandmother."

"Visiting his grandmother?" Becky said.
"That's not fa— ... that's not ... Oh! I see.
 A grandmother isn't like chocolate cake, is she?"
"Certainly not," said Ben's father.

"Any mail for me?" Becky asked.
"A letter for your mom and two for your dad
 and Bert's wildlife magazine.
 Nope. No mail for you," said Mrs. Dash.
"Is no mail for me an elephant's knees
 or chocolate cake?" Becky asked.
"It's no mail," said Mrs. Dash.

"Here's your magazine, Bert," Becky said.
"Is it fair that I didn't get any mail
and everyone else did?"

"Sure," said Bert. "It's as fair as an elephant's knees."

"Come on, Bert," said Becky and Bert's father.
"I'm going downtown and I'm taking you..."
"I'll be fast as a fox," said Bert.

"That's <u>not</u> fair," said Becky.
"A trip downtown <u>isn't</u> an elephant's knees.
It <u>is</u> chocolate cake.
I haven't been downtown for weeks and weeks and
weeks and you went two days ago.
No fair."

"I'm older than you. O-L-D-E-R older," said Bert.
"And wise as an owl."
"That's not fair either," said Becky.

"Let's go, Bert. Now," said Becky and Bert's father.
"I've just got time to get you to the…

... barber for your back-to-school haircut."

"Rats!" said Bert. "That's not fair."

"It <u>is</u> fair!" said Becky.
"As fair as fair as an elephant's knees.
Fair. Perfectly fair."